THE SELFIE BOY AND OTHER SHORT STORIES

Sriramgokul Chinnasamy

First Published in 2022

Becomeshakespeare.com

One Point Six Technologies Pvt Ltd
119-123, 1st Floor, Building J2, B-Wing,
Wadala Truck Terminal, Wadala (East),
Mumbai 400022, Maharashtra, India
T: +91 8080226699

ISBN - 978-93-5610-203-3

For my mum, dad, and brother

Acknowledgements

All the short stories in this collection were written as a part of the final project and various modules while doing my Creative Writing MA at Teesside University, UK. I am greatly indebted to my tutors Sophie Nicholls, Bob Beagrie, Andy Willoughby and Chris Thurgar-Dawson. Without them, this collection wouldn't be possible. I extend my thanks to my publisher BecomeShakespeare, and also to my friend Thaamaraikannan.

About the Author

Sriramgokul Chinnasamy studied Creative Writing MA at Teesside University, UK. He lives in Chennai, India. His poems have appeared in magazines and anthologies in the UK (Envoi, Live from Worktown, The Ash), the US (Poetry Bay), Ireland (Blue Nib), Singapore (Kitaab Online), Canada (The Muse) and India (Muse India, Bengaluru Review).

The Selfie Boy and Other Short Stories is his first book.

Contents

1

THE SELFIE BOY

Fogboro is a medium-sized town you wouldn't have heard of, if you haven't travelled much in the north of England. It's already half-December. There's no snow on the ground but you can't leave your overcoat at home. Apart from Christmas, what does this month remind you of? Shopping! Of course. Don't your children whisper in your ears for storybooks, Minion- or Frozen-themed clothes and toys, before they go to bed now-a-nights? How is it possible that your wife is still calm when she hasn't been giving you any hints of the jewels she's been dreaming about?

Then what are you still waiting for? Take them to the Old Street Shopping Centre, whose entrance faces the Bus Station entrance. Unfortunately, you can't, you idiot, because you are working there at that Old Street! That fourth shop on the left of the entrance is the Smart-Fone shop. That is where you have been employed all year. Now it is Christmas time. Can you even imagine your boss meekly gifting you a day off! Impossible, isn't it? Even if he is willing to, do you have enough money for shopping? Poor you. No day off. But you can double or triple your money, so at least your family goes shopping, while you can tell them over the phone what and what not to buy.

Stop dreaming. You are only halfway through, and the shop is still closed. You have those keys in your jeans pocket. At 9 AM, it's hard to judge the day's crowds, but the man playing violin in Central Square has collected lots of pound coins in front of him. This time yesterday, he had only two or three coins.

Reach the shop, then illuminate it, tidy it, top-up the racks with mobile cases. Do it as early as possible. You are expecting loads of customers and tons of cash from today on. Today is Saturday and the only weekend before Christmas, that is trailing in four days. The management in Newcastle knew your two hands are not enough to meet this upcoming rush. So just three days ago, they hired a young university student on his Christmas vacations to give you a helping hand.

He carried a navy-blue Indian passport. Even though you have a red British passport, you are ethnically a Pakistani. But still, with him you feel like someone from your neighbourhood is working with you.

He was a bit different. You are already fed up of working alone for most of the year and expected someone who will throw proper words at your silent ears, but he spoke only three sentences in the last three days, apart from work issues. Even if you tried to encourage him to speak or smile, he gave you only a single smile or a sentence.

You can't call him dumb. He never sat when he worked, and mostly roamed in the showcase area doing some good sales, especially selling selfie sticks and speakers with inbuilt water fountains. If he got stuck or couldn't understand customers, he never bothered to disturb you in the middle of your phone repairs and billings. Please, forgive him. He is new to this work and might be working for the first time in his whole life. Even if he had worked, he could not have stayed for more than two months in a single job.

He spoke so little. Something was going inside his brain that made him look highly disturbed. He was normal only when he spoke to customers. During the rest of the time, he wandered within the shop like a man without emotions. You are wrong here. People like him are highly emotional, which you can't see with plain eyes. You should become his good mate to understand him better. But, that's not possible in this age, as you made him mop the floor twice so far. Even at his home, he does the mopping only when his parents are out of town and then too, only behind closed doors. You have also made him involuntarily distribute shop pamphlets to the shoppers. These two things will always keep you and him at a distance, and make him wonder whether he should quit this job.

His mind-set is evident from his dressing. You have asked him at least twice from the day he joined to wear full black, but he never bothers to buy black clothes as he's not sure how long he'll be staying and chooses to wear clothes and shoes that are just a tad black.

Around 11 AM, an almost twenty-year-old female walks past him and reports to you for the first day of her work at the Smart-Fone. She was the one whom you had recommended for this job to your Newcastle boss, without knowing her, but knowing only her parents. Anyways, she doesn't know you are married, and from now on, you will never disclose it to her. She carries a red passport. You take photo clicks of it in your smart-cam and send them to your boss. She is officially starting from now on.

"Bro, meet our new employee," you call out to the Indian boy.

"Hello, I'm Ajay," he says in his own tone.

"Myself, Reshma. Where are you from?" She is curious.

"India... And you?"

"Pakistan."

A moment of silence, and you too wonder why she told her ethnicity instead of her nationality, hiding her British passport from his sight.

"What do you study at the university?" You try to fill in the gaps.

"Master's in Fine Art," he answers.

"What's that?" You have never heard of this before.

"It's a study of Painting and Contemporary Art Practices at a higher level."

"I have heard people say, they go to uni to study Computer, Engineering, Medicine, but you say Painting!"

With silence, Ajay goes to attend a customer and sells a selfie stick.

Your silent ears with a lonely year, and three days with the three-sentence speaker, are rescued by Reshma. She has a long tongue, without any shortage of words. Your ears feel blessed now. She, unlike him, loves this job, which is evident from her dressing in full black on her very first day. She sees this job as a source of pocket money and small savings. You know she is likely to aim for longer term work with this shop. Can't you see she is exactly the opposite of him in every single aspect?

Her first day ends, and you have finished giving her a little training required for the job. Reshma and Ajay have not spoken much to each other. The next day, the line that keeps them both apart starts to fade, and yet the line exists. You are in a great astonishment to see him smile his first proper smile, and a big credit for that should be given to her. Till afternoon, they help each other at work even though they themselves struggle separately. You give them both separate lunch timings, yet they recommend food shops to each other and each chooses to eat at the place where the other ate their previous day's meal. Late afternoon, the crowds go dead. They both keep themselves occupied by topping up racks with cases and ordering them. While you do repairs, you can't tolerate them bonding like someone they've known for ages on their very second day. You keep calm, knowing that however thin the dividing line between them may fade, the line will exist because of the ethnic differences they have, and it may grow broader at any instant of time.

You still keep listening to their chats.

"So, how good are your paintings? Are they good as Picasso's and Leonardo's?"

"I'm just a beginner, to be honest," he answers laughing aloud.

"Where do you live?" She waits.

"Fogboro."

"Obviously. Where in Fogboro. Near Linthorpe Road?"

"No! Near to Temple Street. And you?"

"Near the park."

"The one near the mosque?" He awaits her reply.

"Yeah, the same one. What time you finish today?"

"Half-fourish," he replies.

"Same as mine. Let's walk home together."

"Sure," he smiles. "Do you work here full-time?"

"Full-time only during the Christmas holidays. Later, I will be here only on the weekends."

"Which uni are you in?" He looks into her eyes.

"I'm not in uni. Just doing my college, final year."

"Aw, good."

You see her struggle to place the iPhone diamond mobile-cases on the top shelf. When Ajay notices, he kindly takes them from her and reaches the shelf without making any effort to stretch his foot.

Meanwhile a customer visits the shop and starts looking at the water dancing to the tune of the water speakers. You know him very well. He smiles at you, and you give him one back. He is a Brit-Asian in his late forties.

You see Ajay reach to that customer – folding his forehands, and his face and chest leaning by a smaller degree frontwards – with a pleasing tone: "Excuse me, can I help you?"

You find that customer stare at him and say, "No." So, Ajay takes four steps backwards. The customer steps towards you and has a little chat. Then, he summons both Ajay and Reshma.

"Could you both guess who I am?"

"Yeah, might be the boss from Newcastle," Ajay replies.

"Without any doubt, I'm the boss. Are you alright with the job, Reshma?"

"Yes I am," she replies.

"How long have you been working here?" The question to Ajay was harsh.

"Four days," he answers.

"Didn't anyone inform you of the dress code?"

"Yes."

"Then, why the hell are you dressed in grey? The next time I see you informal, you are fired."

Ajay stands silent.

"Unfold your hands, and don't lean forward. You are not a damn hotel waiter serving food over here. Speak aloud. Remember, customers will never buy from you if they can't understand you ..."

Ajay turns blank to the boss's words that continue for five more minutes. There is no use feeling pity for him now. The boss leaves to inspect the other two units of Smart-Fone, at the East End and the River End. You should have alerted him to the boss's arrival, but you deliberately didn't. Look what happened because of you. He is surely going to quit. There is no need for you to bother, if he has to quit at any normal time. But, during Christmas week when the normal shop that makes a profit of £300 a day jumps further to £1500, you can't afford to lose him since there is no time left to train any new worker, and you being the Manager of the three units will be struck with a headache if he leaves.

You see him standing at the corner doing nothing after the boss left. He isn't attending customers. When Reshma tries to console him, her attempts fail. Yet, she understands him and takes extra effort in serving every customer on his and her behalf. You see her hear from Ajay about his decision to quit, and she makes every effort till half-four to make him stay.

Then, they both walk out leaving you in the shop. After an hour, you find them both having milk-chocolate cookies and hot chocolate in Greggs. The shopping bags in Ajay's hands tell you that Reshma has convinced him not to quit, by helping him purchase the necessary clothing for his work. You want him to stay for sake of your business, but why would she!? Stop worrying about business, you fool! Couldn't you see something locks them together on their second day, ignoring all the ethnic barriers they possess, which you lack even after having two kids with your wife or with anyone you ever met. Money is only a need for survival but love is a magic without which humanity won't even exist.

Next day, he arrives wearing full-black clothing. You see his face blush for the first time with an eagerness to work, but you heartless brute, you give him a shock by shifting him permanently to the East End unit.

You make an attempt to build a wall between them, but this is age of tech, you fool. Green and white iPhone messages fly back and forth between the two units. She takes every single opportunity to visit Ajay's unit when your shop runs short of stock. Meanwhile, Ajay creates opportunities to visit your shop whenever he feels like. You deliberately give them both different closing timings, yet they wait and meet for a walk.

Shah, the other employee working with Ajay at East End unit, informs you of Ajay's increasing popularity with the crowd. They even start calling him the Selfie Boy.

Ajay sells dozens of selfie sticks daily, yet you never agree him as the Selfie Boy, until the Christmas Eve, when he bargains and buys from you the last selfie stick left in entire Fogboro. It is pink in colour, and which male would like to have himself a pink one!? You are sure for whom it is bought for. At least, for a proposal with a selfie stick, wouldn't it be that apt to call him the Selfie Boy.

2

ILA

Is it the 4'o clock or 11'o clock bus you are travelling on?

You are a jogging addict. Even the extreme weather can't stop you and your Labrador from running on the early morning streets, with your Labrador's chain firmly in your hand. But what would happen if the hand on the chain gets reversed?

The City of OldFord's Airport is full of crowds, already exceeding its bearing and handling capacity. The officials are struggling hard and doing their level best to keep everything under control. Animals from all around the globe are busy booking their best means of transport as per their budget to reach this city. Most of the tickets are already sold out. The next two days will be even busier. The Mayor is afraid that there are not enough hotels in the city to accommodate so many animals, despite opening four temporary villages in the outskirts that can accommodate 10 million animals each. The expected turnout for the Sapiens Sunday Festival is estimated to be 100 million animals.

Celebrity couple Kevin Rabbit and Celina Parrot are expected to arrive tomorrow. Henry Giraffe, Eliza Penguin, Samuel Kingfisher and Lisa Ape are also expected tomorrow. World Leaders John Eagle, Her Excellency Diana Lioness, Alfred Kangaroo and Tiger Singh are expected on the day of the festival.

This year's festival has turned out to be a sensational hit, even before it begins. The TV rights for live telecast have been sold at record prices. The expected global audiences are said to surpass the count of the recently concluded Olympics.

Despite opposition from Animal groups for Human rights, the clothing retailer Skins has launched its new clothing range made from teenage human skins. Its well-planned launch ahead of this festival is paying well, as four out of every six animals are found arriving at OldFord wearing the Skins brand. The Save Humans campaign is going on at the arrivals hall in all ports and stations, throughout the city and online. Though this campaign attracts some attention, it fails drastically in front of the hype that the festival has created.

Officer Zebra's flight is delayed by half an hour. Top officials are gathered to receive him. Do you know, you are that Officer Zebra they are expecting? But you live on a plane of the universe that is human-dominant. How is that possible for you to switch planes between a human-dominant world and an animal-dominant world?

Everything is possible if you are a first timer to London.

Your boyfriend has boarded a flight to his home country from Heathrow Terminal 4. Heartbreak, right? Memories of your one year relationship keep disturbing you, right? Should be hard to cope – not only for you but for any girl at the end of her first true relationship. Your heart ends up in an emotional jam. Your phone network receiver goes dead as a result of you trying to contact him while you travel on the London tube.

What are you going to do now? You are travelling alone in London with a phone that's temporarily barred from using calls or internet. How are you supposed to find your way back to the hotel? Before you reach your hotel, you have planned to visit Kipling's grave in Westminster Abbey. It was the last place you and your boyfriend have visited together. To reach there, you will have to switch lines between Piccadilly and District lines at Earl's Court tube station. Can you do it and reach Westminster station? Also, you should mind the gap. Do not lose your Oyster Card!

At Abbey's shop, you buy milk chocolates for your 'gone' boyfriend to give it to him when he returns, if he does. Then you reach Victoria station, walk to Belgrave road, remembering the route you have walked for the past two days. Still no aid from your phone. You sign out of the hotel and set off for Victoria bus station. There isn't much time left to catch the bus to York. The horrible taxi driver dropped you at Victoria train station instead of the bus station. You travel round and round the train station instead of reaching the bus station, and there is no one out there to help a first-timer finding her bus. Somehow, you reach the bus station, but the bus driver isn't patient enough to wait till you arrive.

What now? You have missed your 4'o clock bus. Your next bus is at 11 PM. Luckily, the cashier doesn't charge you the full ticket price for the next bus, but only an addition of £5 on top of your old ticket. Your purse is empty now. Anyways, you have your bank card, so don't worry. So you have seven more hours to spend in London before you set off for home. Find a good bar nearby, raise the glass to your boyfriend and drink to kill your worries. But you are hungry; first feed yourself with food before letting alcohol take over.

Wait a minute! Your card shows you are left with zero balance. Where has £2000 gone? Agh, yes. They are safe in your account that isn't linked to the card you are carrying. No cash to withdraw, though you have enough money. Don't worry, you can do an online transfer between your accounts or can contact the nearest branch of your bank. Remember banks close by 5 PM sharp, which is still a few ticks away. Your phone has just now recovered from the network problem it had, but now dies out of charge. There are charging points available at the station at the cost of £2.50, but how much do you have in your pocket? £1.50. Poor girl. Aww, you!

You need internet to transfer money to withdraw cash. For internet, you need to charge your phone, and for charging your phone, you need money. A pound shortage in hand teaches you the value of a pound now. Everything is interlocked now; nothing can be done. You have to spend the remaining six hours inside this bus station doing nothing, except just thinking of your 'gone' boyfriend.

Why not step out of the station and explore some possibilities? What can you expect to do in the City of London with just £1.50 to spend six hours' time? Step out anyways. Wonders can happen only if you step out and try, even if the probability of hope is 0.0001%.

You try to walk back to the hotel you have stayed, in hope of getting help from the receptionist to charge your phone. But, it's risky. Fear of getting lost again stops you. At least you need to find a place to spend time or charge your phone free of cost. Victoria Library, nearby to your bus station, comes to your rescue.

You approach the library desk with your Uni ID card.

"Hello, can I use those computers?"

"Yes, of course. But first, you should be a member of this library," the librarian replies.

"I'm not, but I would like to be. Is there any joining fee?"

"No," he says. And you murmur to yourself "Ah, thank god."

He gives you a membership application form with four pages to fill.

"Should I fill in all the four pages?" asks your doubt-filled voice.

"Yes, if you want to borrow books. Else, only the first page is fine."

So, you fill Ila against your name, 23 against your age, then, female, Student, your home address, phone number and your e-mail.

"Here is your library card. System 9 is reserved for you. It will be available in half an hour and the library closes by 8 PM," informs the kind librarian.

Thanking him, you move to the book shelf titled 'Mystery' on the first floor. *Travelling The Planes* is the book you pick; someone has already bookmarked a page with a 9-spade playing card. That page has the instructions for you to try, and you are curious reading them.

You hear from the librarian that your system is ready to use. You log into the system by scanning the bar code in your library card against the sensor. First, you should complete the task you have come for; transfer the money you need in between your accounts. No one is around you in the library's computer area. You still wonder whether you should give a try to the instructions in the book. You take a deep breath. You look around, gaze at your watch and ask yourself why shouldn't you try it?

Immediately, you scan the 9-spade card against the sensor. A game window pops up on your desktop screen. It asks you to wear the headphones connected to the computer. You do. It requests you to choose an animal character; you fancy a zebra from the options available. So now, you are that Officer Zebra, so much awaited at the OldFord Airport.

Your soul is a human, but not your body. How does it feel to be a Zebra? Fitted in full-formal suiting with goggles, shoes, walking on two legs, carrying a briefcase in one hand and a mini-iPad in the other. Formal greetings from other animal officials are over. Mr Ian Duck is your personal assistant and will take care of you for the next three days. Mr Duck escorts you to one of the oldest Victorian hotels. On the way, you can see the whole town getting decorated for the upcoming Sapiens Sunday Festival. From the window of the church-top-like hotel room, you keep looking at the modern civilized animal-run city. Mr Duck leaves, informing you about the schedules planned for next three days.

Day 1, Mr Duck takes you to inspect the farm factory. This thousand-year-old city has a lot of histories to tell, and this farm factory is a unique example. MileWalk, the centre street of OldFord, runs one mile long, downhill from the King's Castle to the East Peak Cliff and is one of the top rated historic tourist attractions. Every animal knows that MileWalk & Co is one of the finest producers of human meat and dairy. But most of them are not aware that this company operates a farm factory in the underground of historic MileWalk.

In thousands of dungeons, human babies are locked in for the selection process. Female babies are rarely rejected, and the ratio of male babies rejected at this stage is very high. All the rejected babies are taken out of the dungeons and loaded onto a conveyor. Babies don't even know why they are being loaded and where they are being sent. Yet, all of them have innocent looks and enjoy the conveyor ride. Then all of sudden, as few children start to cry, the rest also panic and start to cry out of fear. The conveyor unloads them into a drum of grinders, in which the highly engineered shaft blades that are rotating at a 2,000 rpm grind every child to death.

Those children who escape by falling off the conveyor are noticed by the employed crocodiles, who beat the babies to death by smashing their skull against the floor. Poor babies flutter for at least fifteen minutes in pain of their cracked skulls before they die.

At least the rejected ones suffer the pain for fewer minutes, but those selected babies will undergo the pain of a lifetime. Ostriches carry the selected male babies in wheelbarrows to hand them to buffaloes in the surgery room. Then, the buffaloes with the sharp knives cut the testicles of male babies, without giving any anaesthesia. Aren't their hearts made of muscle? Are their ears deaf to high-pitched cries of the newborns? Mr Duck justifies this act by saying that humans grown for flesh don't deserve testicles. Mr Duck laughs, and then he defends saying that this process will enrich each baby with enormous flesh as one grows up.

"This is barbaric!" You stare at Mr Duck.

"Delicious, was the term you used at dinner table last night," Mr Duck mocks you.

"Is that not ham?"

"That was hum, meaning human. By the way, what is ham?"

"Ah, I mispronounced. Forgive me God, for my unknown cannibalism!"

"What!"

"Nothing. Please don't supply me with hum anymore."

"Okay. But let me see for how long."

What happens to the selected females? Their case is no less in cruelty to the males. They lose their tongues when they are young. Mr Duck tries to justify this, but you are not willing to hear. As they grow up, based on their ability and case study, they are segregated into two categories. One for diary, the other for meat. Those selected for diary are artificially inseminated for breeding younger ones. When they start to lactate, they are injected with a blue injection that increases their milking capacity by blocking the nutrients that are essential for their own survival. This causes, unusual swelling in the milking glands, enormous pain and quicker loss of lactating capacity. But, as long as they can lactate, this injection guarantees whiter and healthier milk for consumers. Once their lactating capacity is gone, those females are immediately beaten to death and buried.

The meat females are given a green injection that leaves their legs paralysed and their breasts begin to swell. Artificial pain is induced into the females for at least half a year before they are taken to the slaughter rooms. The chief priority of the farm remains to satisfy their animal consumers with better leg and breast pieces.

At the slaughter rooms, both males and females for hum and chick, are hung upside down; automated machines are used to slaughter them. The conveyor moves them in inverted position to various machines that rip their body parts, even when they are at their conscious, fully aware of the pain they undergo at each step. Employed animals and machines kill them cruelly inch by inch. The hardest pain is to be ripped apart while enduring the agony. You blurt out your opinion – either kill them in one go or make them unconscious through injection, before slaughtering. They are seen only as a flesh, but there are nerves connected to their flesh too. Why don't animals realise it? Most of the world is speaking against hanging and electric chair as a punishment for crime. Yet, in countries where this is still practised, there are maximum time limits for execution. Why the sense of pain is not considered when it comes to the pain involved with a different species? Your views impress Mr Duck, but he has no powers to stop any of this.

Day 2, Mr Duck takes you to the festival. You have still not recovered from what you had seen on day 1 and wonder about the possibilities of day 2. You are seated in a stadium, with a capacity to seat ninety thousand animals, to witness the inaugural event of the festival. The stadium's west end is open. The 200-meter running track ends at the open West Cliff. One hundred participants can run a single heat.

The King Hen of OldFord waves off the flag; the first round of Sapiens Sunday Festival begins. One hundred humans bought from the different regions of the world are lined up on the track for the first round. Then each of them is splashed with crude oil, and set on fire. On hearing the shot of the gun, they start to run, their bodies engulfed in flames. As they run, three laser lines run along with them. The green line is the life line; whoever can go past it can live. The yellow line denotes the leader in the current festival; the red line denotes the world record time. There are automated glass blockings installed at the finish line. All those who at least passed the green line are allowed to jump of the West Cliff to reach Rr. Hodu and de-flame themselves. But the standard is so high that only five of the participants in round 1 pass the green line. Those who couldn't are blocked at end line and burned to death while the spectators cheer on seeing them die.

There are 83 rounds to be conducted on a single day. Each round will contain ninety thousand new animal spectators and hundred new human participants. The animal that owns the winning human participant of each round gets £1000 as cash, and overall winning owner gets a cheque of £1 million. All the humans who jumped off the cliff are taken to human reserves. The overall winning human is given a free recovery skin surgery sponsored by the famous Skins brand and then taken to human reserves.

Day 3, your last day of the tour. You should submit your inspection report to the King in his castle at MileWalk. You and Mr Duck wait at the King's court for his arrival. While you prepare yourself for the presentation, King Hen arrives and takes his chair. He asks you to summarise your whole report in two minutes.

You request him to ban the Sapiens Sunday Festival on the grounds of human rights. Any act of killing or harming any species for sport should be strictly prohibited. Farming humans for meat and dairy can be accepted on the grounds of the food chain, but the way they are grown and techniques of slaughter should be regulated with human right considerations, with a few recommendations such as painless killing, the right to live in an ethical and natural way until they live, and treatment as a living creature and not solely as a factory input and output product. A strict enforcement of cruelty laws and regular checks to ensure that they are strictly followed.

As you finish, King Hen beaks concern that he has doubts on your genuine animal status. He asks you to prove by answering the simple question, "Which animals are the Adam and Eve of the Animal Kingdom?"

The question shocks you. "Ape and Chimpanzee" is the answer you give. But none of them around is impressed. All the animals start to shout "Alien in disguise!" in a chorus and keep on repeating until the King gives orders to kill you. There are at least a thousand animals within the castle, more than thousands on the roads of MileWalk. You would need to tackle them all alone to reach the South Cliff to escape out of this world. You have only one laser gun with you. It will turn every animal you shoot into an animal with real-world power, which means it's advisable to shoot birds but not violent animals such as tigers and lions. Here is where your game starts and you have only five lives to successfully complete this game. You can choose one animal as your helper, so you choose your favourite Labrador for this task. In the real world, you go jogging every morning with your Labrador, but here you have to sprint, fight and do all sort of gamming stunts to escape from this gaming animal world. Can you do this? Will you make it to the South Cliff within your five given chances? Hopefully. Game set, on your way now.

You wake up in the middle of your bus journey to York from London. Curiously you check to see your watch whether it is the 4'o clock or 11'o clock bus you are travelling on. It is, of course, the 11'o clock bus. You can't remember anything like you jumping the cliff, entering the real world's system 9 of Victoria Library, reaching Victoria station and boarding the 11'o clock bus. Did all this really happen, or did you just have a good sleep on the table of system 9 dreaming about some animal fantasy land and caught the bus back after you woke up? Whatever may be the case, didn't you learn something from what you saw? Start to campaign for animal rights to speak for the animals who can't speak for themselves. Take the responsibility when someone needs you to speak for them. Will you? Please. Though you are a hard core non-vegetarian, you can still make a voice for them.

The bus stops for a food break. You are at the counter of Chicken Bucket Shop.

"Can I have a full veg meal, please?"

"Are you a vegan?" asks the young lady taking orders.

"No, but trying to be."

"Good luck. It will be a five-minute wait for the food to get prepared. Is that okay?"

"Yeah, that's fine."

"It's £4.50 for your meal. Cash or card?"

Paying her with your card, you donate the £1.50 from your pocket into an animal charity box kept at the counter.

This might be the first veg meal you have paid for, at your favourite Chicken Bucket Shop.

3

ACCIDENT, FROM A FOREIGNER'S EYE

Even if all the roads, signals, cars and pedestrian crossings are as good as new, sometimes, things can go wrong and tough things can happen.

My friend and I are heading out of the cinema, after watching the much anticipated movie of the week, in which the hero faces at least six major car accidents and still manages to walk unharmed. Impractical, yet cinematically enjoyable.

While walking down the stairs, eating our leftover popcorn, my friend reacts in an abnormal way after reading a news feed on his phone.

"Lucas is dead! In a car crash in California," he shocks me.

"No way! Please check again, it might be a fake one."

"It's authentic. Even BBC confirms!" he shows me his phone.

Lucas is the hero of the movie that we have just finished watching. By now, everyone coming out of the screens knows about it. Lots of girls immediately go into tears hearing their heart throb is dead. Silence prevails as we walk out.

His death is so ironic; a hero, known for cars and races, dies while racing in his car! This stirs everyone's emotions much deeper than his death could have by any other means.

When we cross the box office, this particular movie's tickets are selling at a rate that no tickets are available for the next two weeks.

Five early-teenagers, unguided by the company of an adult, move out along with us. They quarrel among themselves in naming Lucas' best movies so far, and listing the number of girlfriends and marriages he's had.

While those kids are busy talking, one girl among them keeps calm. She is English, with long black straightened hair, slightly shorter than the others of her age, and carrying a Baskin-Robbins ice cream. In spite of having a runny nose, she inhales often and is keen on finishing her ice cream. She takes a quick glance at me, aware of me noticing her, and then hides her ice cream from my sight as if I'm going to steal it.

When we pass the main exit door, most of the crowd accompanying us takes a right, heading towards the car park. We, along with a handful of people in the company of these kids, take a left, as we all share the joy of walking the roads.

It seems that a shower has just gone by, leaving the roads wet, raindrops dripping here and there. The summer afternoon's temperature has gone down. The winds feel like a winter wind. Half of those handful people with us leave in search of a taxi. Yet, my friend and I, along with the kids and four others, still walk the roads. We are all dressed in our summer clothes, none had a hint of this rain, so we have to pay for not carrying a coat with us. The kids are the least bothered. They are all only dressed in shorts and tees, and still comfortable walking in the winds. That girl is still spooning her ice cream.

We all wait at the signal for the pedestrian's green light to go on. The cars that speed make noises specific of tyres running on wet roads. The tyres splash a fine spray, but the waters vanish before they reach us. That girl is still fighting with her ice cream box.

We all cross one half of the road and wait to cross the other half, as the second half's pedestrian's light is still red. Those teenagers don't have enough patience and successfully walk across the second half. The girl who is busy with ice cream fails to notice them crossing. Suddenly, she realises they are gone and runs into the road without checking for cars – all she wants is to get reunited with her friends, from whom she just disconnected.

Before she ran, she was at my side, within a hand's distance. I could have pulled her and made her stop. But I have missed. If anything is to happen to her now, it is going to be because of my hesitance in stopping her. No use of worrying now; she is half-way, unaware of the speeding car that the green light has given full freedom to. I pray for her. I try to close my eyes but it happens before me.

The car, at a speed impossible to stop in time, tries to stop. The brakes arrest the wheels, yet the speed and the wet road drag the car forward with the tyres making their distinctive screeching sound. The front bumper of the car hits the girl's hip and throws her metres away. Her beloved ice cream box rolls over on the road at least fifteen times, spilling the ice cream all around. The rain and the cream together make scribbling patterns. Her basic Nokia phone spreads in three directions as separate battery, cover and body. Her plastic bag, with a birthday greeting, gifts and a bar of white chocolate, lies near to a gutter.

My friend was on his phone; he never captured the incident till the impact happened. Neither did the four, standing behind. I alone had seen this collision in minute detail. An accident happened, involving a driver who drove as per the rules and a girl whose ignorance and impatience made her risk the wet road.

She lies near the side rails, luckily without bleeding. The people from the nearby bar and the pizza place are now surrounding the spot. All the cars on that side of the road have stopped immediately. The man who drove the car that hit her, parks, turns on the hazard warning lights and arrives at the scene. The girl's friends are standing at the corner, watching the happenings. A woman and a man are trying to wake the girl up by tapping her chin. Thank god! She is alive. She drinks the offered bottle of water.

"Are you alright?" asks the woman.

The girl nods her head, turns around and looks at her spilled ice cream. Then her eyes search for her friends. She finds them, and gives them a smile.

"Can you walk, love?" enquires the woman.

The girl nods yes, and tries to get up. She walks with the help of the woman and the man. She struggles for the first five steps and then walks fine. They make her sit on a bench. Meanwhile, I pick up her bag and deliver it to her, and a lady gives her the Nokia phone with the parts re-attached. She thanks us both. The girl's perfect manners, even during her period of mental recovery after an accident, are astonishing! She switches on her phone and confirms that it is working fine, then hides it in her pocket, thinking the phone is not safe in front of these many gathered strangers.

She might seem to be well at this instance, but she is not. The mental shock in her is still alive; her eyes reflect it. That woman is really a kind-hearted angel. She is helping that girl recover with her healing voice.

The girl looks at her friends, gets scared that they would leave her here and walk home.

So, the girl pleads to the woman, "I need to go home."

"Can you walk home? Are you feeling any pain in your legs?" enquires the woman.

"I am okay... I need to go home," the girl answers, looking at her friends.

"Were you hit by the railing?" the woman asks, checking the child's head.

"I don't know."

"Did she get hit by the railing?" the woman asks the crowd.

"She got hit by the car, might be a minor hit but she needs attention, as she might have injured her hip," is my answer.

"Did you see it?"

"Yes I did."

"And what about the railing?"

"Luckily, she missed it."

After hearing from me the impact of the collision, the man starts to call the ambulance, and the woman consoles the girl that she will be taken home after finishing a small check-up. She starts to cry, wanting to go home. I understand the looks of the girl and the car owner towards me, as if my words are responsible for further hold ups for them both.

By now, I start to realise, where is the friend of mine who accompanied me out of the cinema? Is he gone? No, he is still on the phone, standing at the corner watching things unfold. He waves at me and taps his stomach. We leave the spot to find some good take-away.

4

ANTA

Almost a month back, my husband Noyce had a strange dream. Since then, he turned into someone totally new. He did strange alterations to our home. He filled our bedroom with paintings and pictures of children who have serious looks. The toys and dolls are also frightening. They keep staring at me all day and night, as if they knew what my husband is expecting from me.

Anta is one of those toys. He is a foot tall, with blue eyes and curly hair. While I was pregnant, Anta was a gift from my husband. Later, I had a miscarriage and lost my son. Anta has been the one with whom I can feel the presence of my missing child. But he is always asleep. I know he is a toy. My grief needed healing, and he became my temporary remedy.

Noyce doesn't want my pain to fade. He keeps his pain and expects the same from me. I have been in some sort of bondage since his dream. Bondage with open doors and windows. No ropes to tie, or keys to lock me in. No one to guard me, nor any force to stop me from running away. I am always open to walk out, but it is both a willing and unwilling bondage.

Noyce spoke in a very kind voice. He requested me to agree for what he wanted. He fed me food with spoons, and sometimes with his very own hands, when he turned overemotional.

He has been too kind – a type of kindness that I think is poisonous.

At one point I have to give up to his month-long, kind and persuading words that penetrated my ears to reach my brain and heart, to make them both come in sync with his wish. Which woman on earth doesn't care for her lost child or lost motherhood? What he asks is impossible to accept, not only for me but for anyone in my situation. A belief is still common in a world we live in, that women undergo maximum pain during child birth. But, try asking any woman who has lost a child during her pregnancy; she would definitely disagree. Even with such a pain in me, why am I not still bending for what he is expecting from me? If I can't bend for him now, he can't even imagine me doing that for the rest of my life. So, now I am ready to do what he wants, for the sake of our future child.

My state of refusal gets shattered. For the past few days, while he spoke his kind words, he kept stroking and tickling Anta. Though his actions seemed soft, the emotions they stirred in me were violent. I saw his soft strokes on Anta like that of him twisting Anta's head cruelly left and right. His tickling action on Anta provoked me to think he is stabbing Anta continuously for six or seven times. I couldn't tolerate him doing anything to Anta, so I give up.

Noyce's left hand waits for me to place my right hand over his palm. He then pulls me out of my sitting position with a single force, slowly guiding me out of our bedroom towards the bathroom. As he fills the tub with water, waiting for it to reach a level, he starts to undress me. When I'm naked, he turns me around, gathers my falling hair that reaches till my 12th vertebra, and knots it into a single globe on my head. He doesn't bend me at this instance; instead, he gives me a feathery push that lands me inside the tub. Another small push with his right hand on my front and a little hold with his left arm on back of my neck forces me into the tub of water in a flat position.

He folds his pants till knee-level, and twists his wrist watch. His watch shows 12'o clock, but it doesn't show that it is midnight. His insanity is at peak. He uses only cold water to fill this tub, never bothering of the hot-water pipe that is still in a perfect working condition. Freezing! But it's just a small fraction of the difficulty that I'm to experience from now on.

He places his one foot on the floor, and the other on top of me, in-between my breasts. Holding my skull, he drowns me into the water. For around half a minute, I remain, holding my breath. I was a swimmer when in school, so I had previous experiences of being under water for a long time. I can tackle this kind of situation better than most normal people can. Yet even for me, it is not so easy as he is executing his insanity in this damn freezing water at this damn odd time. In less than a minute, my eyes start to feel the pain in its corners. Icy waters reduce my capacity to control my breath. As a result, I start to struggle for life inside the water like a fish battling for life on ground. I strain my eyeballs to see his watch, but only two minutes have passed. I start to panic, bubbles rush out of my nose and mouth like a fire from an insane dragon. My mouth goes wide open, wanting to get some air. Pressure starts to build within my ears, heart and brain. The water storms through my throat, and a little of the water back-pedals through my nose.

My knotted hair unfolds and spreads like floating black algae, while its tips pierce my nose and eyes. I'm no longer able to resist. My limbs are fast fluttering. My body tries to thrust upwards, but his masculine right leg floors me. As a last hope, I use my sharp nails to wound his throat, causing some bloodshed. My energy dies, and I go motionless and half-unconscious. I don't even know how long I was inside. But when he frees me, I don't reflex back with a fierce wake up, nor am I breathing hard-core. Instead, I remain drowned showing no movement, even after the much-needed release.

He then picks me out of tub with care, drops me slowly on to the floor, giving me all necessary first aid to pump the water out of my lungs. Then, he wipes my wet skin and hair with a soft towel. On return of my consciousness, I'm lying on the bed, dressed in comfortable clothes. The heating is also turned on to the maximum. He is drying my hair with a hair dryer. Such care from the same hands that were hurting me so badly, just a few minutes back.

I could see the wounds on his neck, which I am responsible for. He gives me a smile, and so do I. Kissing my forehead, he grasps my hands and starts to shape my nails with a cutter, so no harm can be done to him again. Deeply thanking me for my co-operation in the tub, he has started to spell his silent word passages, which I keep listening as usual.

After an hour or so, he covers my head with a plastic bag. The mouth of the bag is tied around my neck with a belt, so that no air moves in or out. The only gap that enables me to breathe is a hole of small radius, placed thankfully near to my nose. I am to spend this full night wearing this bag. My hands are chained to prevent me from removing the bag. Usually, this kind of sleeping is extremely suffocating, but after having such a terrific breathing tub exercise, this seems very easy to adapt.

Both of these exercises would be killing me almost every day for the coming month, but my ability to sustain without air for a long time will improve, especially when the radius of the breathing hole in the plastic bag reduces by a bit every single night.

We are not in an isolated location, where my voice or shouts will not be heard. It is a place where surely our neighbours can hear. He has my consent. I will assist him despite the agony I undergo. I will never betray the faith he has in me. Looking forward to that one day, for which my exercises are preparing me for.

***

It all began with the dream Noyce has had. But a day before his dream, I was warned about the possibility of him having a morbid dream. When he was away for work, I had two visitors – Mr. and Mrs. Jimbell.

Mrs. Jimbell was Noyce's ex-mistress.

Once all the guest formalities were over, Mrs. Jimbell empathised, "I heard that you had a miscarriage recently. My prayers are with you."

I cared less for her words, so I gave a short answer: "Three days ago, in a much unexpected way."

"I can imagine the pain, because I too had lost my child before breaking up with Noyce," she shocked me.

"Really! Sorry. I never knew anything of that. I was only aware that you both were in a relationship."

"I have only short time left, before which I have to warn you," she spoke in a hurried voice.

"Warn me about what?"

"About the dream."

"What dream?"

"Sooner or later, he will let you know of it."

"I understand nothing, Mrs. Jimbell."

"Listen carefully. When I lost my child, Noyce believed that he has got a curse which prevents him from having a baby. He might believe the same in your case as well. He will talk to you about a dream and how to eliminate this curse."

"What is the dream about? If that's true, I have no issue with helping him with it."

"It is not that easy, Madame. First, let me warn you the consequences of saying no. See how I look now? This is the result of walking away from Noyce."

She looked like someone with a serious skin disease. Even though she'd covered herself enough, her exposed hands reflected the nature of her extremely skin-affected body. She'd lost most of her hair, and there was heavy dandruff in her scalp. Her make-up made her face look okay, but little efforts of make-up on her neck showed the reflection of her true face, horrible even to imagine.

"Look at my husband, Mr. Jimbell. A clever man when I married him, but he has lost his mind now," she cried.

Mr. Jimbell kept counting his £5 coins, again and again, in and out of the metallic coin holder, right from the time he'd stepped in.

"How is my husband to be blamed for all this?" I voiced out my anger.

"You will understand when it's time. He has a lot of friends who are involved with black magic, and he is the one who has cursed me."

"Enough! My doors are waiting for you both to leave."

She warned, "Beware of the dream," and they both walked out.

I had never had a real-life exposure to witches. She was the first witch I had ever encountered. How dare she accuse my husband as someone involved with black magic? She must have been the one involved with those practices, and some of those must have turned back to her. But, I also couldn't ignore her warning. Why did both my husband's children have to end up aborted? Does that mean the curse exists? Or has she used some magic to abort my child, with a deliberate intent to harm Noyce?

That night I was lying in bed thinking – What is the dream going to be about? Will Noyce really have a dream? Did she seed his brain with this dream when they lost their child? But I strongly believe that all these have something to do with my lost child, and will have an effect on the future pregnancies I will have through Noyce. And if I leave Noyce, will I turn into someone just like Mrs. Jimbell?

I kept watching Noyce without a single blink. Is he dreaming what Mrs. Jimbell spoke about earlier? His face started to sweat, and his body kept shivering. He then woke up experiencing some nightmare.

"Are you alright, Noyce?"

"No."

I gave him a hug to make him feel better.

"If I am to bury you under sand, for 15 minutes straight, will you agree and co-operate? I promise I will bring you back alive," he whispered in my ears and shocked me.

"What!" I cried.

"Please! Trust me. I'm not going to let you die …"

This was the moment when he started preparing me both mentally and physically, so I could participate in the burial ritual to help him overcome his curse.

***

Tonight is the much anticipated one; I am going under sand for fifteen minutes, alive. My month-long training makes me confident of withstanding even more. I have reached a point where I want to bury myself more than my husband wants me to, for the sake of bringing back Anta to this world.

At the backyard, around 2 AM, Noyce has just finished digging a six-foot grave for me. He has kept our car in a standby position. The first-aid kit and the oxygen mask are also ready to assist me. These preparations show me that Noyce has a will to rescue me back alive.

I jump inside the grave, and I lay straight and relaxed. He fills the sand on top of me. I keep humming whatever the song that comes to my mind. The weight of sand on my top starts to increase gradually, and all of the sudden, I feel no weight. I get pulled out of the grave. Is it over that quick? No. His love for me suddenly starts to turn into a villain. He back foots at the last minute, fearing about the possibility of my death. If that's the case, where was all his love hiding during the last month? Earlier, when I wanted to jump out of the tub water, his leg pressed me inside. Now when I want to stay inside, why do his hands run for my rescue?

I can see Anta, watching us from a nearby tree. Then he nods his head and starts to walk away, as he understands that we are not ready to struggle for his return. He makes me feel ashamed and guilty. I plead Noyce to give this burial an immediate try, but he is not in a position to listen, because of the sudden return of this shit called love.

I keep calling Anta's name. He hears me but pretends as if he doesn't. There is no point in believing Noyce. I have decided to do the most myself. I hit Noyce on his head with a shovel. Well, this is a calculated hit, hoping that he will not stay unconscious for more than a quarter of an hour. I start to load my little sand truck with all the sand required to cover me up. Positioning the truck near the grave, I lay inside the grave with the remote to control the sand truck.

Anta, I know you will walk back. Don't hide yourself from top of my grave; I can see you peeping. Come on, show me your face before I get filled in with sand. He slowly moves his childish face forward and wishes me good luck.

Using the remote, I empty the sand truck all in one go, filling the six-foot grave I am lying in. I'm not sure whether Noyce can return to consciousness within the expected time. If he does, the curse would get eliminated and I will be delivering him Anta, the very next year. And if he doesn't, I will be meeting my Anta in his very own world. Whatever may be the case, no one can stop me from meeting my Anta.

5

REPLACEABLE

My bloody alarm won't stop ringing till it wakes me up. Even before looking for time, I check for the notifications on the locked screen of my phone. Are there any texts from her? None. Has she woken up? Let me see. FB messenger & WhatsApp show she was online an hour ago. Today, she didn't start the texting. Probably because she has got nothing to get done from me today. Otherwise, by now, her messages would have bombarded my inbox. Okay, let me start the texting.

6:15 AM

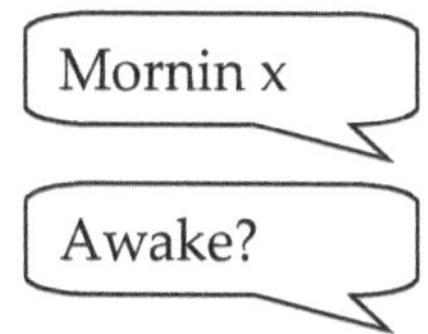

Both the messages are unseen.

After waiting patiently for 45 minutes, I'm about to start getting ready for work. Now, two FB messages pop with their specific ding sounds. Should I go to the bath or pick the phone?

7:00 AM

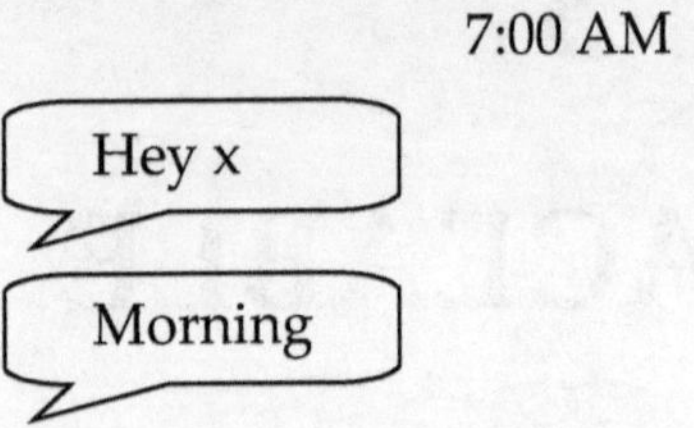

Seconds later, two more messages pop up.

Not much of a difference
You've sold burgers and fries earlier
Now gonna sell gifts and greeting cards instead :-p
Erm...There is a big difference
Lol
Well from today on, I might not be able to speak to you like b4

Are you breaking up with me?

Not like that, love

It's bcoz of my new job.

I just want to shift my full focus to work

So that I can be on the current job for longer

Okay

It's up to you

I should hurry up now. I end up taking a long shower than usual. In 10 minutes, I manage to leave home, perfectly neat in my bookstore uniform. I stop for a coffee and sausage roll on the way. Walking for about half an hour, I reach the bookstore on time. Facing my bookstore is her Burger Shop. As she no longer works there, it seems kind of deserted to my eyes. I miss her hi-byes and the little chats, now and then from across the road.

A week has passed. I wait for her messages to pop up, at least on weekends when she isn't working. But there is no word from her. For some reason, I too don't feel like initiating the messages after we had our last chat. A series of misunderstandings and quarrels with her in the last month keep haunting me.

I know where she resides and where she currently works. I can go and show up. But a part of me warns that she is not into me anymore. With all the confusions in me while walking home, I end up near the Parmo House. It was the place where we both went on our first date. Recently, we had even celebrated our Valentine's Day over there. In less than two months, in the same spot, I see her on her date with her new boyfriend, both kissing each other. I leave from there immediately to find a good place to drink.

Next day, at work, I face the blues from the previous night. I don't feel like eating. But I don't want to waste my lunch break sitting inside the bookstore. So, I choose to eat at the Burger Shop where she used to work.

While I'm standing in the queue to give my order, memories of the past go passing me. When I came here for the first time, she was the one who took my order. I still remember the order I gave: Chicken Burger, Nuggets and Latte. The second day she shocked me by repeating my previous day order, without me even saying a word. From the next day on, Latte was ready when she saw me in the queue and the rest were ready by the time I reached the counter. Some days I feel like choosing something different from my usual menu, but she didn't even allow me to give the order. She made orders herself, as per what she wished me to eat. This is how all it started.

Now, after knowing she has moved on, none of these memories matter.

Taking a coffee and burger from the girl who replaced my ex at work, I find a better spot in the dining area. There is a tissue paper beneath my coffee cup with a message, "Hey x catch me up here around 6." The new girl serving at the counter smiles at me and winks. I raise the coffee cup as a gesture, agreeing to meet her.

FORTHCOMING PUBLICATION

A Teesside Girl and Other Poems

A poetry collection

by

Sriramgokul Chinnasamy

PreeTa Press

Bolton, UK

2022

www.ingramcontent.com/pod-product-compliance
Lightning Source LLC
LaVergne TN
LVHW041436170726
843492LV00008B/2626